The Fa

The Princess Tales

The Fairy's Mistake

Gail Carson Levine

ILLUSTRATED BY Mark Elliott

SCHOLASTIC INC.

New York Toronto London Auckland Sydney
Mexico City New Delhi Hong Kong

ISBN 0-439-17911-4

12 11 10 9 8 7 6 5 4 3   0 1 2 3 4 5/0

Printed in the U.S.A.   01

First Scholastic printing, May 2000

Cover design and typography by Michele N. Tupper

ALSO BY
Gail Carson Levine

Ella Enchanted

THE PRINCESS TALES:
The Princess Test

All my thanks

to my wonderful editor, Alix Reid.

Without you, *The Princess Tales*

would never have been told.

—G.C.L.

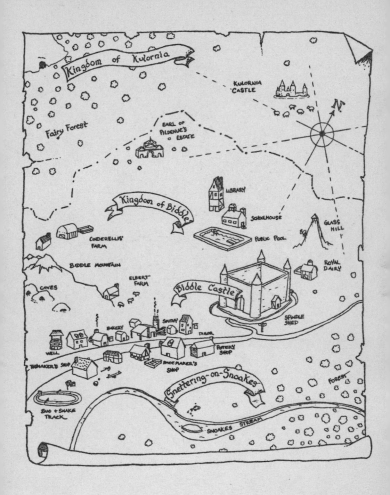

One

Once upon a time, in the village of Snettering-on-Snoakes in the kingdom of Biddle, Rosella fetched water from the well for the four thousand and eighty-eighth time.

Rosella always fetched the water because her identical twin sister, Myrtle, always refused to go. And their mother, the widow Pickering, never made Myrtle do anything. Instead, she made Rosella do everything.

At the well the fairy Ethelinda was having a drink. When she saw Rosella coming, she changed herself into an old lady. Then she made herself look thirsty.

"Would you like a drink, Grandmother?" Rosella said.

"That would be lovely, dearie."

Rosella lowered her wooden bucket into the well. When she lifted it out, she held the dipper so the old lady could drink.

Ethelinda slurped the water. "Thank you. Your kindness merits a reward. From now—"

"You don't have . . ." Rosella stopped. Something funny was happening in her mouth. Had she lost a tooth? There was something hard under her tongue. And something hard in her cheek. "Excuse me." Now there was something in her other cheek. She spat delicately into her hand.

2

"SHE SPAT DELICATELY INTO HER HAND."

They weren't teeth. She was holding a diamond and two opals.

"There, dearie." Ethelinda smiled. "Isn't that nice?"

Two

"What took you so long?" Myrtle said when Rosella got home.

"Your sister almost perished from thirst, you lazybones," their mother said.

"I gave a drink to . . ." Something was in Rosella's mouth again. It was between her lip and her front teeth this time. "I gave a drink to an old lady." An emerald and another diamond fell out of her mouth. They landed on the dirt floor of the cottage.

"It was more important— What's that?" Myrtle said.

"What's that?" the widow said.

They both dove for the jewels, but Myrtle got there first.

"Rosella darling," the widow said, "sit down. Make yourself comfortable. Now tell us all about it. Don't leave anything out."

There wasn't much to tell, only enough to cover the bottom of Myrtle's teacup with gems.

"Which way did the old lady go?" Myrtle asked.

Rosella was puzzled. "She didn't go anywhere." An amethyst dropped into the teacup.

Myrtle grabbed the bucket and ran.

When she saw Myrtle in the distance, Ethelinda thought Rosella had come back. Only this time she wasn't tripping lightly down the path, smelling the flowers and humming a tune. She

6

was hurtling along, head down, arms swinging, bucket flying. And then Ethelinda's fairy powers told her that this was Rosella's twin sister. Ethelinda got ready by turning herself into a knight.

"Where did the old lady go?" Myrtle said when she reached the well.

"I haven't seen anyone. I've been alone, hoping some kind maiden would come by and give me a drink. I can't do it myself with all this armor."

"What's in it for me if I do?"

The fairy tilted her head. Her armor clanked. "The happiness of helping someone in need."

"Well, in that case, get your page to do it." Myrtle stomped off.

Ethelinda turned herself back into a fairy. "Your rudeness merits a punishment," she said. But Myrtle was too far away to hear.

Myrtle went through the whole village of Snettering-on-Snoakes, searching for the old lady. The villagers knew she was Myrtle and not Rosella by her scowl and by the way she acted. Myrtle marched into shops and right into people's houses. She opened doors to rooms and even closets. Whenever anyone yelled at her, her only answer was to slam the door on her way out.

While Myrtle was in the village, Rosella went out to her garden to pick peas for dinner. As she worked, she sang.

Oh, May is the lovely month.
Sing hey nonny May-o!
Oh, June is the flower month.
Sing hey nonny June-o!
Oh, July is the hot month.
Sing hey nonny July-o!

And so on. While she sang, gems dropped from her mouth. It still felt funny, but she was getting used to it. Except once she popped a pea into her mouth as she sang, and she almost broke a tooth on a ruby.

Rosella had a sweet voice, but Prince Harold, who happened to be riding by, wasn't musical. He wouldn't have stopped, except he spotted the sapphire trembling on Rosella's lip. He watched it tumble into the vegetables.

He tied his horse up at the widow Pickering's picket fence.

Rosella didn't see him, and she went on singing.

Oh, November is the harvest month.
Sing hey nonny November-o!
Oh, December is the last month.
Sing hey . . .

Prince Harold went into the garden. "Maiden . . ."

Rosella looked up from her peas. A man! A nobleman! She blushed prettily.

She wasn't bad-looking, Prince Harold thought. "Pardon me," he said. "You've dropped some jewels. Allow me."

"Oh! Don't trouble yourself, Sir." Another sapphire and a moonstone fell out of Rosella's mouth.

Harold had a terrible thought. Maybe they were just glass. He picked up a stone. "May I examine this?"

Rosella nodded.

It didn't look like glass. It looked like a perfect diamond, five carats at least. But if the gems were real, why was she leaving them on the ground? He held up a jewel. "Maiden, is this really a diamond?"

"I don't know, Sir. It might be."

A topaz hit Prince Harold in the forehead. He caught it as it bounced off his chin. "Maiden, have jewels always come out of your mouth?"

Rosella laughed, a lovely tinkling sound. "Oh no, Sir. It only began this afternoon when an old lady—I think she may have been a fairy—"

They *were* real then! Harold knelt before her. "Maiden, I am Prince Harold. I love you madly. Will you marry me?"

Three

Rosella didn't love the prince madly, but she liked him. He was so polite. And she thought it might be pleasanter to be a princess than to be the widow Pickering's daughter and Myrtle's sister. Besides, it could be against the law to say no to a prince. So she said yes, and dropped a garnet into his hand.

"I'm sorry, sweetheart. I didn't hear you."

"Yes, Your Highness."

Clink. Clink. Two more garnets joined Harold's collection. "You must say, 'Yes, Harold,' now that we're betrothed."

"Yes, Harold."

Clink.

The fairy Ethelinda was delighted that Rosella was going to be a princess. She deserves it, the fairy thought. Ethelinda was pleased with herself for having given Rosella the perfect reward.

The widow Pickering agreed to the marriage. But she insisted that Harold give her all the gems Rosella had produced before their engagement. The widow was careful not to mention Myrtle. She didn't want the prince to know that Rosella had a twin sister who would also have a jewel mine in her mouth. After all, what if he took Myrtle away too?

Prince Harold swung Rosella up on his horse. He asked her to hold an open saddlebag on her lap. Then he mounted in front of her. As they rode off, he asked her about her garden, about the weather, about fly fishing, about anything.

"HE ASKED HER ABOUT HER GARDEN. ABOUT
THE WEATHER . . . ABOUT ANYTHING."

The widow stood at the fence and waved her handkerchief. As she turned to go back into the cottage, she saw her favorite daughter in the distance. Myrtle was loping along, swinging the bucket. The widow opened the gate and followed her daughter into the house. "Darling, speak to me."

Myrtle sank into their only comfortable chair. "Hi, Mom. The stupid old lady wasn't—" There was a tickle in the back of her throat. What was going on? It felt like her tongue had gotten loose and was flopping around in her mouth. Could she be making jewels too? Did it happen just by going to the well? Whatever it was— diamond or pearl or emerald—it wanted to get out. Myrtle opened her mouth.

A garter snake slithered out.

The widow screamed and jumped onto their other chair. "Eeeeek! Get that thing out of here! Myrtle!" She pointed a shaking finger. "There it is! Get it! Eeeeek!"

Myrtle didn't budge. She stared at the snake coiling itself around a bedpost. How had this happened if the old lady wasn't at the well? The knight? The knight! The old lady had turned herself into a knight.

Myrtle jumped up and raced out, taking the bucket with her. "'Bye, Mom," she called over her shoulder. "See you later." Two mosquitoes and a dragonfly flew out of her mouth.

The fairy Ethelinda watched Myrtle scurry down the road. She patted herself on the back for having given Myrtle the perfect punishment.

Four

Prince Harold and Rosella reached the courtyard in front of the prince's palace. He lifted Rosella down from the horse.

"I'm too madly in love to wait," he said. "Let's announce our engagement first thing tomorrow morning, dear heart."

"All right," Rosella said.

Harold only got a measly seed pearl. "Princesses speak in complete sentences, darling."

Rosella took a deep breath for courage. "I'm tired. Your High—I mean Harold. May I rest for a day first?"

But Harold didn't listen. He was too

interested in the green diamond in his hand. "I've never seen one of these before, honey bun. We can have the betrothal ceremony at nine o'clock sharp. Your Royal Ladies-in-Waiting will find you something to wear."

Harold snapped his fingers, and a Royal Lady-in-Waiting led Rosella away. They were on the castle doorstep when Harold ran after them.

"Angel, I almost forgot. What would you like served at our betrothal feast?"

Nobody had ever asked Rosella this kind of question before. She'd always had to eat scraps from her mother's and her sister's plates. Nobody had ever asked her what she liked to eat. Nobody had ever asked her opinion about anything.

She smiled happily. "Your—I mean, Harold . . . uh . . . dear, I'd like poached quail eggs and roasted chestnuts for our betrothal feast." Six identical emeralds the color of maple leaves in May dropped from Rosella's mouth.

The Royal Lady-in-Waiting, who was at Rosella's elbow, gasped.

"Look at these!" Harold said. "They're gorgeous. So you want wild boar for dinner?" He didn't give Rosella time to say she hated wild boar. "What do you know? It's my favorite too. I'll go tell the cook." He rushed off.

Rosella sighed.

The fairy Ethelinda, who was keeping an eye on things, sighed too.

⚓ ⚓ ⚓

Myrtle returned to the well, determined to give a drink to anybody who was there. But nobody was. She lowered the bucket into the well anyway.

Nobody showed up.

She had an idea. It was worth a try. She watered the plants that grew around the well. "Dear plants," she began. "You look thirsty. Perhaps a little water would please you. It's no trouble. I don't mind, dear sweet plants."

Whatever was in her mouth was too big to be a jewel, unless it was the biggest one in the world. And a jewel wouldn't feel slimy on her tongue. She opened her mouth. A water bug crawled out. She closed her mouth, but there was more. More slime. She opened her mouth again. Two more water bugs padded out, followed by a black snake.

Giving the plants a drink hadn't done any good. Myrtle dumped the rest of the water on a rosebush. "Drown, you stupid plant," she muttered. A grasshopper landed on a rose.

Myrtle filled her bucket one more

time. Then—without saying a single word—she scoured the village again for the rotten fairy who'd done this to her. She swore to herself that she'd pour water down the throat of any stranger she found.

But there were no strangers, so Myrtle threw the bucket into the well and headed for home.

The widow was in the garden. She had dug up the peas and the radishes and the tomato plants. Now she was pawing through the roots, hoping to find some jewels that Prince Harold had missed. When she heard the gate slam shut, she stood up. "Don't say a word if you didn't find that old lady."

Myrtle closed her mouth with a snap. She picked up a stick and scratched in the dirt, "Where's Rosella?"

"She rode off to marry a prince. And like a fool, I let her go, because I thought I had you. You bungler, you idiot, you . . ."

That made Myrtle furious. How could she have known the fairy would turn herself into a knight in so much armor you couldn't even see her—his—face? And hadn't she searched the village twice? And hadn't she watered those useless plants? Myrtle opened her mouth to give her mother what-for.

But the widow held up her hands and jumped back three feet. "Hush! Shh! Hush, my love. Perhaps I was hasty. We've both had a bad . . ."

Her mother's pleas gave Myrtle a new idea. She picked up the stick again and wrote, "Things are looking up, Mom. It will all be better tomorrow." She dropped the stick and started whistling—and wondering if whistling made snakes and insects too.

It didn't. Too bad, she thought.

Five

Rosella was used to sleeping on the floor, because Myrtle and the widow had always taken the bed. In the palace she got her own bed. It had a canopy and three mattresses piled on top of each other and satin sheets and ermine blankets and pillows filled with swans' feathers.

So she should have gotten a fine night's sleep—except that three Royal Guards stood at attention around her bed all night. One stood at each side of the bed, and one stood at the foot. If she talked in her sleep, they were supposed to catch the jewels and keep them safe for Prince Harold.

Rosella didn't talk in her sleep because she couldn't sleep with people watching her. By morning her throat felt scratchy. She thought she might be coming down with a cold.

Her twelve Royal Ladies-in-Waiting brought breakfast to her at seven o'clock. Scrambled eggs and wild-boar sausages. They shared the sausages while she ate the eggs. Rosella said "please" six times and "thank you" eight times. Each Royal Lady-in-Waiting got one jewel, and they fought over the remaining two.

"Nobody deserves that but me!" yelled one Royal Lady-in-Waiting.

"I work harder than any of you!" yelled another.

"I'm worth ten of each of you, so I should get everything!" shouted a third.

"You have some nerve, thinking . . ."

Rosella put her hands over her ears. She wished she could have ten minutes to herself.

Prince Harold came in. He coughed to get the attention of the Royal Ladies-in-Waiting. Nobody noticed except Rosella, who smiled at him. He'd be handsome, she thought, if he weren't so greedy.

The Royal Ladies-in-Waiting went on arguing.

"How dare you—"

"What do you mean—"

"The first person who—"

"SHUT UP!" Harold roared.

They did.

"You mustn't upset my bride." He went to Rosella, who was eating her breakfast in bed. He put his arm around her shoulder. "Are you all right, sugar plum?"

Rosella nodded. She liked the pet names he called her. But she hoped he wouldn't make her say anything.

"Tell me so I'm sure, lovey-dove."

The fairy Ethelinda was worried.

⚓ ⚓ ⚓

Myrtle, on the other hand, had a great night's sleep. When she woke up, she put paper, a quill pen, and a bottle of ink in a pouch. Then she set out for the village. She'd have a fine breakfast when she got there, and she wouldn't pay a penny for it. As for the bucket she'd thrown down the well, why, she'd have her choice of buckets.

Her first stop was the baker's shop. She's scowling, the baker thought, so it's Myrtle. He scowled right back.

"Give me three of your freshest muffins," Myrtle said.

"HE SCOWLED RIGHT BACK."

She has some nerve, the baker thought. Bossing me— What was coming out of her mouth? Ants! He grabbed his broom and swept them out of his store. He tried to sweep Myrtle out too.

"Cut that out!" Myrtle said. A horse-fly flew out of her mouth. A bedbug climbed over the edge of her lip and started down her chin.

The baker swatted the fly. He kept an eye on the bedbug, so he could kill it as soon as it touched the floor.

Myrtle took the pen and paper out of her pouch. "Give me the muffins and I won't say another word," she wrote. "I also want a fourteen-layer cake. It's for my party tomorrow, to celebrate my fourteen-year-and-six-weeks birthday. You're invited. Bring the whole family."

The baker swallowed hard and nodded. "I'll come. We'll all come. We'll be, uh, overjoyed to come." He wrapped up his most delicious muffins. When he handed them to Myrtle, he bowed.

The fairy Ethelinda was getting anxious. Punishments weren't supposed to work this way.

⚓ ⚓ ⚓

Rosella tried not to talk while she got ready for her betrothal, but her Royal Ladies-in-Waiting ignored her if she just pointed at things. They didn't yell at each other anymore, because they didn't want Prince Harold to hear, but that didn't stop them from fighting quietly.

When Rosella said, "I'll wear that gown," two amazon stones and an opal fell to the carpet. And the twelve Royal Ladies-in-Waiting went for the jewels, hitting and shoving each other.

So Rosella took the gown out of the

closet herself and laid it out on her bed. Then she stood over it, marveling. It was silk, with an embroidered bodice. Its gathered sleeves ended in lace that would tickle her fingers delightfully. And the train was lace over silk, yards and yards of it.

"It's so pretty," she whispered. "It belongs in the sky with the moon and the stars."

Two pearls and a starstone fell into the deep folds of the gown's skirt. They were seen by a Royal Lady-in-Waiting who had taken a break from the fight on the carpet. She pounced on the gown.

The other Royal Ladies-in-Waiting heard the silk rustle. They pounced too. In less time than it takes to sew on a button, the gown lay in tatters on the bed.

Rosella wanted to scream, but she was afraid to. Screaming might make bigger and better gems. Then she'd have to scream all the time. Besides, her throat was really starting to hurt. She cried instead.

The fairy Ethelinda was getting angry. Rewards weren't supposed to work this way.

Six

Rosella didn't mean to, but she dropped jewels on every gown in her princess wardrobe except one. And her Royal Ladies-in-Waiting ruined each of them. The one that was left was made of burlap and it was a size and a half too big. It didn't have a real train, but it did trail on the floor, because it was four inches too long.

Harold met Rosella in the palace's great hall, where the Chief Royal Councillor was going to perform the betrothal ceremony. The prince thought she looked pretty, with her brown wavy hair and her big gray eyes. But why had she picked the ugliest gown in the kingdom? It was big enough for her and a gorilla. All he said, though, was, "You look beautiful, honey bunch. Are you glad to be engaged?"

Rosella didn't know how to answer. Being engaged wasn't the problem, although marrying Harold might have its drawbacks. The problem was the jewels.

"Did you hear me, hon? I asked you a question." He raised his voice. "Are you happy, sweetheart?" He cupped his hand under her chin.

Rosella spoke through her teeth so the jewels wouldn't get out. "Everybody wants me to talk, but nobody listens to what I say."

"I'm listening, angel. Spit it out."

"I hate wild boar, and I don't want guards to stand around. . . ." There were so many jewels in her mouth that one popped out, a hyacinth.

Harold put it in his pocket. The orchestra started to play.

She couldn't keep all these stones in her mouth. She spit them into her hand and made a fist.

"We're supposed to hold hands," Harold whispered. "Give them to me. I'll take good care of them."

What difference did it make? She let him have them.

The ceremony began.

Myrtle sat on the edge of the well to eat her muffins. After she ate them and licked her fingers, she headed for the stationer's shop. When she got there, an earwig and a spider bought her enough party invitations for everyone in the village. At the bottom of each invitation she wrote, "Bring presents."

She gave out all the invitations, and everyone promised to come. Then she stopped at the tailor's shop, where she picked out a gown for the party. It was white silk with an embroidered bodice and a lace train.

She was in such a good mood, she even bought a gown for her mother.

The fairy Ethelinda was furious.

⚓ ⚓ ⚓

At the end of the betrothal ceremony, the First Chancellor placed a golden tiara on Rosella's head. She wondered if she was a princess yet, or still just a princess-to-be.

"Some people want to meet you, honey," Harold said.

After a Royal Engagement, the kingdom's loyal subjects were always allowed into the palace to meet their future princess.

The Royal Guards opened the huge wooden doors to the great hall. Rosella saw a line that stretched for three quarters of a mile outside the palace. Everyone in it had something to catch the jewels as they cascaded out of her mouth. Pessimists brought thimbles and egg cups. Optimists brought sacks and pillow-cases and lobster pots.

The first subject Rosella met was a farmer. "How are you?" he said.

"Fine." A ruby chip fell into his pail.

That was all? His shoulders slumped.

Rosella took pity on him. She said, "Actually, my throat hurts, and this crown is giving me a headache."

He grinned as stones clattered against the bottom of his pail. Rosella asked him what he planned to do with the jewels.

41

"My old plow is worn out," he said. "I need a new one."

"Do you have enough now?" she said.

"Oh yes. Your Princess-ship. Thank you." He bowed and shook her hand.

Next in line was a woman whose skirt and blouse were as ragged as Rosella's had been yesterday. The woman wanted to buy a warm coat for the winter. Something about her made Rosella want to give her diamonds.

Rosella said, "Make sure your new coat is lined with fur. I think beaver is best." Diamond, she thought. Diamond, diamond.

But only one diamond came out, along with a topaz, some aquamarine stones, and some garnets. Thinking the name of the jewel didn't seem to make much difference. Anyway, the woman caught the stones in a threadbare sack and left happy.

A shoemaker came next, carrying a boot to catch the jewels. "What's your favorite flower?" he asked.

"Lilacs and carnations and daffodils," Rosella sang, wondering if singing would affect what came out—a diamond, a ruby, and a turquoise on the large side.

The shoemaker said he had been too poor to buy leather to make any more shoes. "But now," he said, "I can buy enough to fill my shop window."

Rosella smiled. "And peonies and poppies and black-eyed Susans and marigolds and—"

She was starting to get the hang of it. Long vowels usually made precious jewels, while short vowels often made semiprecious stones. The softer she

43

spoke, the smaller the jewels, and the louder the bigger. It really was a good thing she hadn't screamed at her Royal Ladies-in-Waiting.

"That's enough. Don't use them all up on me."

Rosella wished Harold would listen to this shoemaker. He could learn something.

Even though her throat hurt, she enjoyed talking to everybody. She liked her subjects! But why were so many of them poor?

Next was a boy who asked her to tell him a story. She made up a fable about a talkative parrot who lived with a deaf mouse. The boy listened and laughed in all the right places, and caught the jewels in his cap.

She smiled bravely and said hello to the next subject. Her throat hurt terribly.

Seven

The widow Pickering loved her new gown. She tried it on while Myrtle tried on her own new gown. The widow told Myrtle that she looked fantastic. Myrtle wrote that the new gown made her mother look twenty years younger.

They took off the gowns and hung them up so they wouldn't wrinkle. Then Myrtle went out into the yard to experiment. She hummed softly. A line of ants pushed between her lips. She hummed louder, and the ants got bigger. Even louder, and the ants got even bigger. She'd had no idea there were such big ants. These were as big as her big toe.

Enough ants. Myrtle opened her mouth wide and sang, "La, la, la, la. Tra lee tra la tra loo." Moths, fireflies, and ladybugs flew out.

She hummed again. This time worms and caterpillars wriggled out. Hmmm. So she didn't always get ants by humming.

She tried speaking. "Nasty. Mean. Smelly. Rotten. Stupid. Loathsome." She giggled. "Vile. Putrid. Scabby. Mangy . . ."

They were crowding out—crawling, flitting, slithering, darting, wriggling, whizzing, oozing, flying, marching—escaping from Myrtle's mouth every way they could.

There were aphids, butterflies, mambas, lacewings, lynx spiders, midges, wolf snakes, gnats, mayflies, rhinoceros vipers, audacious jumping spiders, bandy-bandy

"THEY WERE CROWDING OUT—
CRAWLING, FLITTING, SLITHERING."

snakes, wasps, locusts, fleas, thrips, ticks, and every other bug and spider and snake you could think of.

Myrtle kept experimenting. She had a wonderful time, but she didn't figure out how to make a particular snake or insect come out. All she learned was that the louder she got, the bigger the creature that came out.

After about an hour, she had worked up quite an appetite. So she and her mother went to the village to have dinner at the inn. Dinner was free, because the innkeeper wanted to keep Myrtle from saying one single solitary word.

The fairy Ethelinda was scandalized.

⚓ ⚓ ⚓

During the betrothal banquet Harold noticed that Rosella's voice was fading. He noticed because all he got were tiny gems, hardly more than shavings. So he didn't make her say much. But he did make her drink wild-boar broth.

"It's the best thing for you, tootsie," he said when she made a face.

She gulped it down and hoped it would stay there. She picked at her string beans. "Why are your subjects so poor?" she whispered. A tiny sapphire and bits of amber fell onto the tablecloth.

Harold brushed the jewels into his hand. His betrothed was sweet, but she didn't know much. Subjects were always poor. "I wish they were richer too, cutie pie. Then I could tax them more."

"Maybe we can help them." A pearl fell into Rosella's mashed potatoes.

Harold dug it out with his fork and rinsed it off in his mulled wine. "Honey, you'll wear yourself out worrying about them. Take it easy. Relax a little."

She fell asleep over dessert. Royal Servants carried her to her bedchamber. But she woke up when the three Royal Guards took their places around her bed. Then she couldn't fall back to sleep.

Eight

Myrtle and the widow Pickering slept late the next morning. When they woke up, they strolled to the village. They stopped at the toymaker's shop for favors for the party guests. From the potter they ordered serving platters. The butcher promised them sausages and meat pies. By noon they had picked out everything for the party. Then they linked arms and sauntered home.

The fairy Ethelinda gnashed her teeth.

⚓ ⚓ ⚓

By morning Rosella's throat hurt worse than ever. She thought she had a fever, too. But her voice was stronger.

Breakfast was wild-boar steak and eggs. Before her Royal Ladies-in-Waiting had taken ten bites, Harold sent for her.

He was waiting in the library. As soon as she went in, she became very scared. There were thousands of books, but they weren't what scared her. She liked books. There were four desks. That was fine, too. There were a dozen uphol-stered leather chairs, and they looked comfortable enough. A Royal Man-servant and a Royal Maid were dusting. They were all right.

The terrifying sight was the fifteen empty chests lined up in front of one of the leather chairs.

"Sweetie pie," Harold said. "Am I glad to see you." He led her to the chair behind the empty chests. "Wait till I tell you my idea."

Rosella sat down.

"Did you have a good breakfast, cuddle bunch?"

It hurt too much to talk. She shook her head.

Harold was too excited to pay attention. "Good. Here's my idea. You've noticed how old and moldy this palace is?"

She shook her head.

"You haven't? Well, it is. The draw-bridge creaks. The rooms are drafty. The cellars are full of rats. The place should be condemned."

She didn't say anything. The palace looked fine to her.

"So I had a brainstorm. You didn't know you were marrying a genius, did you?"

She shook her head.

"This is brilliant. Listen. We're going to build a new castle. That's my idea. Picture it. Cream-colored stone. Marble everywhere. Hundreds of fountains. Taller towers than anybody ever heard of. Crocodiles *and* serpents in the moat. People will travel thousands of miles to see it. You'll be famous, sweetheart."

"Me?"

Harold caught the tiny ruby. "Yes, you. I can't build a palace on current revenues. We need your voice. The kingdom needs you. So just make sure they land in the chests, will you, sugar?"

She was silent.

"I know. You're wondering how you'll ever think of things to say to fill fifteen chests. That's why we're in the library. All you have to do is read out loud. Here." He pulled a book off a shelf. "This looks interesting. *The History of the*

Monarchy in the Kingdom of Biddle. That's us, love." He put the book in her lap. "You can read about our family."

She didn't open it. What could he do to her if she didn't talk? He could throw her in a dungeon. She wouldn't mind if he did. Bread and water would be better than wild boar. Then again, he could chop off her head, which would hurt her throat even more than it was hurting now.

"I know you're tired, darling. But after you fill these chests, you can take a vacation. You won't have to say a word." He got down on one knee. "Please, sweetheart. Pretty please."

He has his heart set on a new palace, Rosella thought. He'll be miserable if he doesn't get one, and it will be because of me. Rosella opened the book to the middle. I'm too kindhearted, she thought.

She started reading, trying to speak around her sore throat. "The fourth son of King Beauregard the Hairy weighed seven pounds and eleven ounces at birth. He had a noodle-shaped birthmark on his left shoulder. He wailed for . . ."

A stream of jewels fell into the chest. Harold tiptoed out of the room.

Rosella went on reading. "The infant was named Durward. His first word, 'More,' proved him to be . . ." She was freezing. She looked up. The fire looked hot. ". . . proved him to be a true royal son. His tutors reported . . ." The room was spinning. ". . . reported that he excelled at archery, hunting . . ." What was wrong with this book? The letters were getting bigger and smaller. The lines of print were wavy. ". . . hunting, and milit—"

Rosella fainted and fell off her chair.

The Royal Manservant and Royal Maid rushed to the partly filled chest. They each grabbed a handful of jewels. Then the Royal Manservant ran to find Harold, while the Royal Maid used her apron to fan Rosella.

"Wake up, Your Highness. Please wake up," she cried.

Nine

The fairy Ethelinda was appalled.
This was the last straw. She had to do
something.

Harold was in the courtyard, practicing
his swordplay. She materialized in front
of him. She didn't bother to disguise herself, hoping he'd be terrified when he saw
the works—all seven feet three inches of
her, her fleshy pink wings, the shimmer
in the air around her, the purple light she
was always bathed in, her flashing wand.

"You're a fairy, right?" Harold said when
he saw her. He didn't seem frightened.

"I am the fairy Ethelinda," she said,

"HAROLD WAS IN THE COURTYARD,
PRACTICING HIS SWORDPLAY."

lowering her voice to a roar.

Harold grinned. "Pretty good guessing on my part, considering I've never met a fairy before."

"I am the one who made the jewels come out of Rosella's mouth."

Harold almost jumped up and down, he was so excited. "That was you? Really? Uh, say, Ethel . . . tell me, what did my sweetie pie do to make you do it?"

"My name is *Ethelinda*," the fairy boomed. "I rewarded her after she gave me a drink of well water."

"I can do that. That's a—"

"I'm not thirsty. Do you know that you're making poor Rosella miserable?"

"She's not miserable. She's a princess. She's deliriously happy."

Ethelinda tried a different approach. "Why do you want jewels so much?"

"You wouldn't want them?"

"Not if it was making my betrothed unhappy."

"How could she be unhappy? If I were in her shoes, I'd be delighted. She wouldn't be a princess today if I hadn't come along. She gets to wear a crown. She has nice gowns, Royal Ladies-in-Waiting. And me."

"You have to stop making her talk."

"But she has to talk. That's what makes *me* happy."

Ethelinda raised her wand. Prince Harold was one second away from becoming a frog. Then she lowered it. Her self-confidence was gone. If she turned him into a frog, he might figure out a way to make it better than being a prince. She certainly didn't want to reward him the way she'd rewarded Myrtle.

She didn't know what to do.

The Royal Manservant who'd seen

Rosella faint finally reached the courtyard. He ran to Harold.

Ethelinda vanished.

⚓ ⚓ ⚓

Myrtle's party started at two o'clock. The
schoolteacher arrived first. His present
was a slate and ten boxes of colored
chalk.

Myrtle opened one of the boxes. She
wrote on the slate in green and orange
letters, "Thank you. I'll let you know
when I run out of chalk."

The baker came next. His cake was
so big that it barely fit through the
cottage doorway. The icing was choco-
late. The decorations were pink and
blue whipped cream. The writing on top
said, "Happy Fourteen-and-Six-Weeks
Birthday, Myrtle! Please Keep Quiet!"

The whole village came. Nobody

wanted to take a chance on making Myrtle mad. The guests filled the cottage and the yard and the yards of the surrounding cottages. The widow thanked them all for coming. Myrtle collected her presents. She smiled when anyone handed her an especially big box.

The food was the finest anybody could remember. Myrtle ate so many poached quail eggs and roasted chestnuts that she almost got sick. After everybody ate, she opened her presents. There were hundreds of them. Her favorites were:

The framed sampler that read, "Speak to me only with thine eyes."

The bouquet of mums.

The music box that played "Hush, Little Baby."

The silver quill pen, engraved with the motto "The pen is mightier than the voice."

The parrot that sat on Myrtle's shoulder and repeated over and over, "Shut your trap. Shut your trap. Shut your trap."

The charm bracelet with the golden letters S, I, L, E, N, C, and E.

After all the presents were opened, everybody sang "Happy Birthday." Myrtle was so thrilled that she smiled and clapped her hands.

⚓ ⚓ ⚓

Rosella was gravely ill, and Harold was seriously frightened. Even under mounds of swansdown quilts, she couldn't stop shivering. She felt as if a vulture's claws were scratching at her throat and a carpenter hammering at her temples.

The Royal Physician was called in to examine her. When he was finished, he told Harold that she was very sick. He said her only hope of recovery lay in bed rest and complete silence. His fee for the visit was the jewels he collected when he listened to her chest and made her say "Aah" sixteen times.

Ten

Myrtle had a birthday party every week. She and the widow laughed and laughed at their silliness in wishing for jewels to come out of Myrtle's mouth. When Myrtle got bored between parties, she would speak into a big jar. Then she'd let the bugs and the snakes loose in the yard and make them race. She and her mother would have a grand time betting on the winners.

Rosella got better so slowly that Ethelinda's patience snapped. The evening after Myrtle's fourth party, Ethelinda materialized as herself in the widow's cottage. "I am the fairy Ethelinda, who rewarded your sister and punished you. You have to help Rosella," she thundered.

Myrtle sneered. "I do? I have to?"

A bull snake slithered under Ethelinda's gown. A gnat bit her wing.

"Ouch!" Ethelinda yelped.

"Be careful, dear," the widow told Myrtle. "You might make a poisonous snake."

"Yes, you have to help her," Ethelinda said. "Or I'll punish you severely."

Myrtle wrote on her slate, "I like your punishments."

"I can take your punishment away," Ethelinda said.

As fast as she could, Myrtle wrote, "What do I have to do?"

Ethelinda explained the problem.

"I can fix that," Myrtle wrote.

Ethelinda transported Myrtle to the palace, where Rosella was staring up at her lace bed canopy and wondering when her nighttime guards would arrive. As Ethelinda and Myrtle materialized, Ethelinda turned herself back into the old lady.

"I've brought your sister to help you, my dear," Ethelinda said.

Rosella stared at them. Myrtle would never help her.

Myrtle had brought her slate with her. She wrote, "Change clothes with me and hide under the covers."

Rosella didn't move. She wondered if she was delirious.

"Go ahead. Do it," Ethelinda said. "She won't hurt you."

Rosella nodded. She put on Myrtle's silk nightdress with the gold embroidery and slipped deep under the blankets.

Myrtle got into Rosella's silk nightdress with the silver embroidery.

Myrtle climbed into Rosella's bed. She sat up and yodeled, long and loud. A hognose snake wriggled out of her mouth.

Harold heard her, even though he was at the other end of the palace. He started running, leaping, and skipping toward the sound. "She's better! She's well again!" he yelled. And how many jewels did that yodel make? he wondered.

Ethelinda made the snake disappear. Then she made herself invisible.

"Precious!" Harold said, coming through the door. He dashed to the bed. "The roses are back in your cheeks. Speak to me!"

"What roses?" Myrtle yelled as loud as she could. "I feel terrible." The head of a boa constrictor filled her mouth.

Harold jumped back. "Aaaa! What's that?"

Rosella lifted a tiny corner of blanket so she could watch. The snake slithered out and wound itself around Myrtle's waist.

Myrtle grinned at Harold. "Do you like him? Should I name him after you?" Three hornets flew straight at him. One of them stung him on the nose. The other two buzzed around his head.

"Ouch! Wh-what's going on . . . h-honey pie? Th-that's a s-snake. Wh-where did the j-jewels go? Why are b-bugs and snakes coming out?"

This is fun, Myrtle thought. Who'd have thought I could scare a prince?

Poor Harold, Rosella thought. But it serves him right. He looks so silly. She fought back a giggle and wished she could make a bug come out of her mouth once in a while.

"I'm angry. This is what happens when I get angry." A scorpion stuck its head out of Myrtle's mouth.

"Yow! Why are you angry? At me? What did I do?"

"It's not so great being a princess," Myrtle yelled. "Nobody listens to me. All they care about are the jewels. You're the worst. It's all you care about, too. And I don't want to eat wild boar ever again. I hate wild boar."

The air was so thick with insects that Harold could hardly see. Snakes wriggled across the carpets. Snakes slithered up the sconces. Snakes oozed down the tapestries. A gigantic one hung from the chandelier, its head swaying slowly.

A milk snake slipped under the covers. It settled its clammy body next to Rosella. She wanted to scream and run.

Instead, she bit her lip and stayed very, very still.

"Sweetheart, I'm sorry. Forgive me. Ouch! That hurt."

Myrtle screamed, "I'M NOT GOING TO TALK UNLESS I WANT TO!"

"All right. All right! You won't have to. And I'll listen to you. I promise." Something bit his foot all the way through his boot. He hopped and kicked to get rid of it. "Everyone will listen. By order of Prince Harold."

"AND PRINCESS ROSELLA," Myrtle yelled.

"And Princess Rosella," Harold echoed.

Myrtle lowered her voice. "Now leave me. I need my rest."

Eleven

After Harold left, Ethelinda made the snakes and bugs disappear. Rosella came out from under the covers.

"Thank you," Rosella told her sister. An emerald fell on the counterpane.

Myrtle snatched the jewel and said, "You're welcome." She snagged the fly before it got to Rosella's face. Then she crushed it in her fist.

"You've done a good deed," Ethelinda began.

Myrtle shook her head. "Don't reward me. Thanks, but no thanks." She let two cockroaches fall into the bed.

Ethelinda asked if Myrtle would help Rosella again if she needed it.

"Why should I?" Myrtle asked.

"I'll pay you," Rosella said.

Myrtle pocketed the two diamonds. Not bad. She'd get to frighten the prince again and get jewels for it, too. "Okay."

Myrtle and Rosella switched clothes again. Then Ethelinda sent Myrtle back home. When Myrtle was gone, Ethelinda said she had to leave too. She vanished.

Rosella sank back into her pillows. She didn't want Myrtle to help again, or even Ethelinda. She wanted to solve the problem of Harold and his poor subjects all by herself.

⚓ ⚓ ⚓

Harold didn't dare visit Rosella again that day. But he did command the Royal Servants to listen to her. So Rosella got rid of her nighttime guards. And she had her meal of poached quail eggs and roasted chestnuts at last.

She also ordered the Royal Ladies-in-Waiting to bring her a slate and chalk. From then on, she wrote instead of talking to them. She was tired of having them dive into her lap whenever she said anything.

And she had them bring her a box with a lock and a key. She kept the box and the slate by her side so she'd be ready when Harold came.

He showed up a week after Myrtle's visit. Rosella felt fine by then. She was sitting at her window, watching a juggler in the courtyard.

"Honey?" He poked his head in. He was ready to run if the room was full of creepy-crawlies. But the coast seemed clear, so he stepped in all the way. He was carrying a bouquet of daisies and a box of taffy. "All better, sweetheart?" He held the daisies in front of his face—in case any hornets started flying.

He looks so scared, Rosella thought. She smiled to make him stop worrying.

He lowered the bouquet cautiously and placed it on a table. Then he sat next to her and looked her over. She seemed healthy. That silk nightdress was cute. Blue was a good color for her.

He hoped she wasn't feeling miserable anymore. Anyone who was going to marry him should be the happiest maiden in the kingdom. He still wanted her to talk up enough jewels for a new palace. Then, after that, he wouldn't mind a golden coach and a few other items. But he wanted her to be happy, too.

They sat there, not saying anything.

"Oh, here," Harold said finally. He held

"THEY SAT THERE, NOT SAYING ANYTHING."

out the bouquet and the candy.

She took them. "Thank you."

An opal hovered on her lip and tumbled out. Harold reached for it, but Rosella was faster. She opened her box and dropped in the opal. It clinked against the stones already in there. She snapped the box shut.

That was pretty selfish of her, Harold thought. He started to get mad, but then he thought of boa constrictors and hornets. He calmed down. "What's the box for, darling?"

"My jewels." A pearl came out this time. A big one. It went into the box too.

"Honey . . . Sweetie pie . . . What are you going to do with them?"

"Give them away. Your subjects need them more than we do."

"NO YOU DON'T!" Harold hollered. She couldn't! It was all right to give jewels away for the engagement ceremony. That was once in a lifetime, but she wanted to make a habit of it. "You can't give them away. I won't allow it."

Rosella wrote on her slate, "I'm trying not to get angry."

"No, no, don't get mad!" Harold started backing away. "But don't you want a new palace? I'll tell you what—we'll name a wing after you. It'll be the Rosella Wing. How do you like that?"

She shook her head. "This palace is beautiful. Look at it! It's wonderful."

All those gems going into the box! thought Harold. Wasted! If she gave them away, soon his subjects would be richer than he was. "Tell you what," Harold said. "We'll split fifty-fifty."

"I won't read a million books out loud just to fill up your treasure chests."

He counted as they fell. Two diamonds,

three bloodstones, one hyacinth, and one turquoise.

He sighed. "All right, my love."

"All right, my love. Fifty-fifty." Rosella wanted to be fair. He had made her a princess, after all.

They shook hands. Then they kissed.

Epilogue

M_{yrtle} never had to come to her
sister's rescue ever again. The fifty-fifty
deal worked out perfectly. Harold got
his new palace and golden coach, even-
tually. And Rosella was happy talking to
her subjects and making sure they had
enough plows and winter coats and
leather for making shoes. Also, she built
them a new school and a library and a
swimming pool.

In time she and Harold grew to love
each other very much. Harold even
stopped trying to steal the jewels from
Rosella's wooden box while she was

sleeping. And Rosella stopped counting them every morning when she woke up.

Myrtle and her mother went into the bug-and-snake-racing business. People came from twenty kingdoms to watch Myrtle's races. They'd bet beetles against spiders or rattlers against pythons or grasshoppers against garter snakes. The widow would call the races, and Myrtle would take the bets. The whole village got rich from the tourist trade. And Myrtle became truly popular, which annoyed her.

Ethelinda grew more careful. Myrtle was her last mistake. Nowadays when she punishes people, they stay punished. And when she rewards them, they don't get sick.

And they all lived happily ever after.

Rosella's Song

Oh, January is the first month.

Sing hey nonny January-o!

Oh, February is the cold month.

Sing hey nonny February-o!

Oh, March is the windy month.

Sing hey nonny March-o!

Oh, April is the rainy month.

Sing hey nonny April-o!

Oh, May is the lovely month.

Sing hey nonny May-o!

Oh, June is the flower month.

Sing hey nonny June-o!

Oh, July is the hot month.

Sing hey nonny July-o!

Oh, August is the berry month.

Sing hey nonny August-o!

Oh, September is the red-leaf month.

Sing hey nonny September-o!

Oh, October is the scary month.

Sing hey nonny October-o!

Oh, November is the harvest month.

Sing hey nonny November-o!

Oh, December is the last month.

Sing hey nonny December-o!